Who Dia It?

Malachy Doyle ✳ Joy Gosney

Picture Corgi

Zeena loves splashing about in puddles.

Archie won't go anywhere without his bear.

Meet the Whodunnit Gang. On every page, one of them has done something silly. Can you find out who it is? You might have to look very carefully for clues!

Sam likes football and spiders.

Emily wants to be a princess.

Max has a little dog called Ruff, who follows him to school every day.

Someone painted the wall.
Who did it?

Can you spot?

blue cap

wheel

big fish
little fish

3 carrots

4 5 6 7 8 9 10

pink paint pot

teddy bear

banana

white rabbit

Can you spot?

green cabbage

wheelbarrow

jumping rabbit

1 very tall sunflower

Someone let the rabbits in with the guinea pigs.
Who was it?

white guinea pig

spotty rabbit

food bag

2 water containers

Someone forgot to drink their milk.

Who was it?

Can you spot?

2 red straws

3 big jugs

cow

4 books

 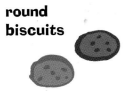

$2 + 3 = ?$

$4 - 1 = ?$

$3 + 2 = ?$

$= 2$

$= 3$

$2 + 3 =$

Can you spot?

red triangle

drum

yellow sun

3 green blocks

Someone drew on the whiteboard.
Who did it?

spotty cushion

round globe

orange marker pen

blue square

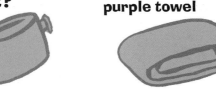

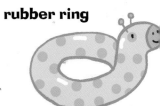

Someone put a load of ducks in the pool.
Who was it?

rucksack

spotty swimming costume

10 ducks

stripey swimming trunks

Can you spot?

dog bowl

3 blue chairs

5 forks

4 cups

Someone was flicking peas.
Who was it?

Someone dug a great big hole in the sandpit.
Who did it?

Can you spot?

pink wellies

diamond shape

scooter

trailer

sandcastle

square bucket

ball

green flag

Can you spot?

feather

tadpoles

brown
socks

beetle

**Someone left muddy footprints
all over the floor.**

Who was it?

magnifying glass

acorn

spider

orange leaves

Someone's gingerbread man isn't even a person.
Whose?

Can you spot?

bag of flour

stripey oven gloves

whisk

measuring jug

Can you spot?

stripey scarf

orange whistle

bucket

blue spade

big bubble

green scrubbing brush

sponge

drying rack

Someone put too much soap in!
Who did it?

Can you spot?

big bowl

2 wooden spoons

checked dishcloth

washing-up liquid

7 eggs

red apron

3 biscuit cutters

rolling pin

Someone buried the football.
Who was it?

2 red flags

loud rattle

3 guinea pigs

7 yellow sashes

Some people made silly faces
in the school photo.
Who?

Bye-bye, Whodunnit Gang!
See you again soon, maybe.

But can you remember who's who?
And can you remember what
silly things they did?

Who painted the wall?

Sam!

Who let the rabbits in with the guinea pigs?

Archie!

Who forgot to drink their milk?

Emily!

Who drew on the whiteboard.

Zeena!

Who put a load of ducks in the pool?

Archie!

Who was flicking peas?

Zeena!

Who dug a big hole in the sandpit?

Max!

Who left muddy footprints all over the floor?

Zeena!

Whose gingerbread man isn't even a person?

Sam!

Who put too much soap in?

Emily!

Who buried the football?

Max!

Who made silly faces in the school photo?

The Whodunnit Gang!